Originally published in Austria in 2018 as *Der Bärenvogelschatz*
Copyright © 2018 by G&G Verlagsgesellschaft mbh, Wien
English translation copyright © 2020 by Laura Szejnmann
First published in Canada, the U.S., and the U.K. by Greystone Books in 2020

20 21 22 23 24 5 4 3 2 1

Greystone Kids / Greystone Books Ltd.
greystonebooks.com

Cataloguing data available from Library and Archives Canada
ISBN 978-1-77164-653-6 (cloth)
ISBN 978-1-77164-654-3 (epub)

Copy editing by Paula Ayer
Proofreading by Antonia Banyard
English text design by Sara Gillingham Studio
Jacket illustration by Stella Dreis

Printed and bound in Malaysia on ancient-forest-friendly paper by Tien Wah Press

Greystone Books gratefully acknowledges the Musqueam, Squamish, and Tsleil-Waututh peoples on whose land our office is located.

Greystone Books thanks the Canada Council for the Arts, the British Columbia Arts Council, the Province of British Columbia through the Book Publishing Tax Credit, and the Government of Canada for supporting our publishing activities.

STELLA DREIS

LITTLE BEAR'S TREASURES

GREYSTONE KIDS

GREYSTONE BOOKS • VANCOUVER/BERKELEY

Little Bear examined his treasures.

A shiny button, tickly feathers, a soft cloud, a handy clothespin, a cozy hiding place, a shy piece of fluff . . .

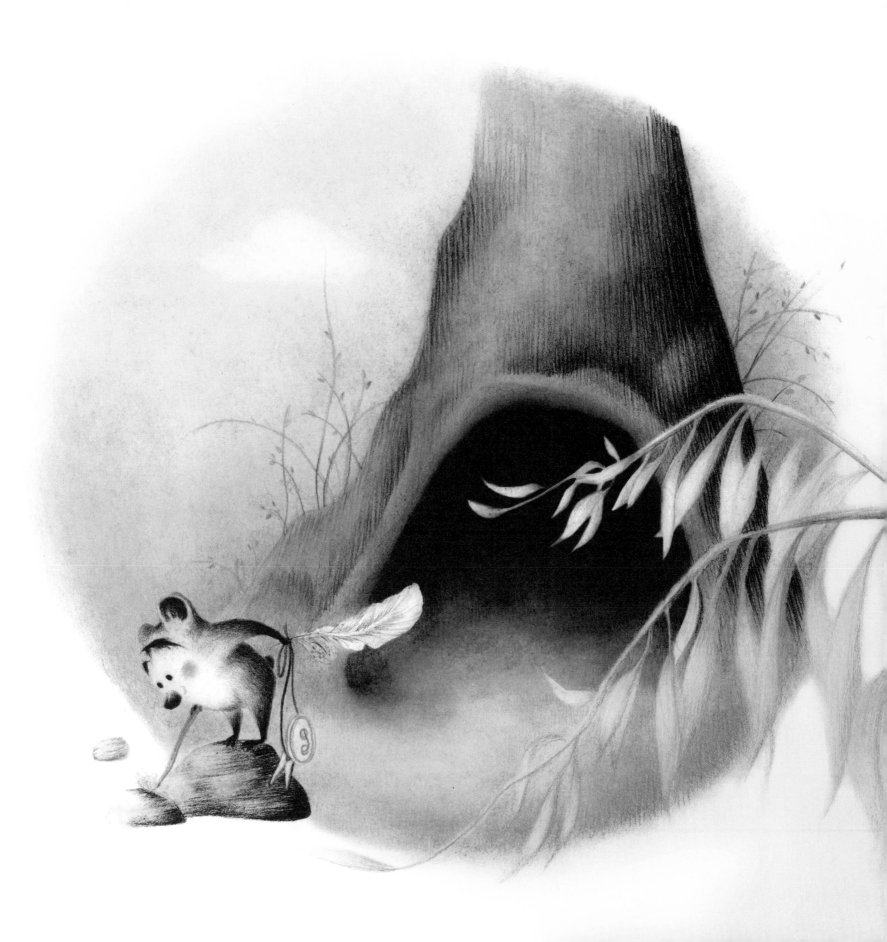

. . . a magic stick,

endless dust to dance in,

and a bush brimming with blueberries.

Wow—so many!

Little Bear hummed happily.

Little Bear was a great treasure finder. That's right, a treasure *finder*, because he didn't *look* for his treasures—he *found* them. Everywhere. And he shared the news about his treasures with everyone he met.

But as hard as he tried . . .

. . . no one listened,
or really understood.

"Treasures?" The other animals shook their heads. "Those aren't treasures. They're just junk."

Eventually, Little Bear stopped sharing. He became quiet and his little nose drooped down low.

He sighed sadly.

"Watch out or your nose will hit a root!" said a voice.

Little Bear jumped. "Who said that?"

"Up here!" piped the voice.

Little Bear looked up.

It was a little bird

on his head!

"What are you doing, with your nose so low?"

Little Bear explained, "I like to find treasure, like . . ."
He pointed. "Like this stick."

"Ooo, a magic stick!" said Little Bird.

Little Bear's nose perked up. Little Bird understood!

"Can I find treasure with you?" Little Bird chirped.

Little Bear didn't need to be asked twice. Off they went.

And, oh, what they found!

Together they discovered:

a tree-bark boat

thinking hats

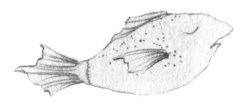

some glittering fish

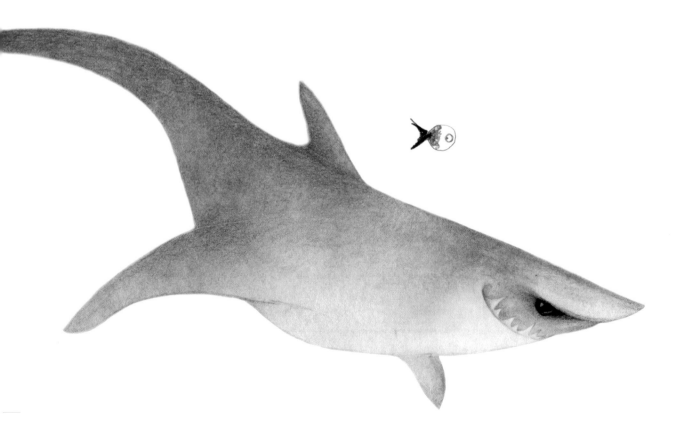

a swingy tree

a bunch of bats

a log for trumpeting

a giant mushroom

a mysterious fog

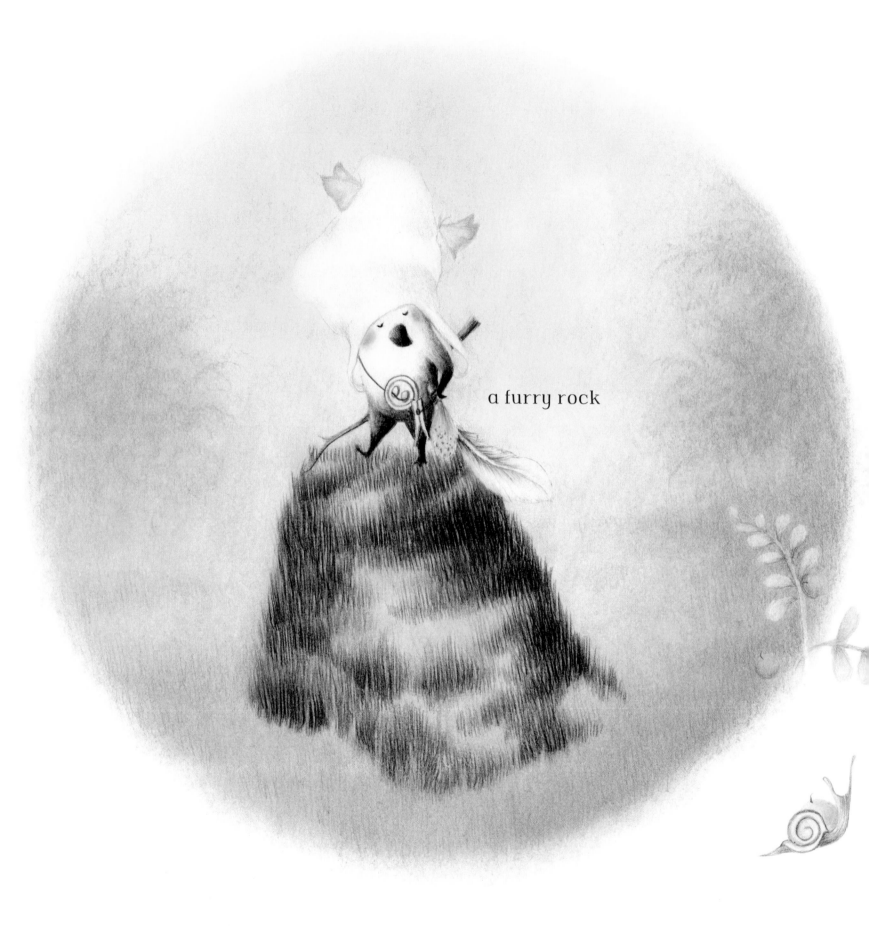

a furry rock

a crown for the bear, and one for the bird.

And so it went on . . .

Because when treasures are shared, they multiply.

Soon nighttime fell. The blossoms tucked themselves
into bed. The sun slipped away to give way to the moon.
And somewhere between the sky and the earth, the
little bear and the little bird stood still.

"Oh!" was all they could say.

This was a true bear-bird treasure!

They stood there like two kings and counted the stars
until Little Bird started to snore.

Little Bear felt like the happiest bear in the whole world.

He listened for a long time, so long that snow—or was

it stardust?—sprinkled his fur, and he thought about

treasure. How you can find treasure. How treasure can

find you. How the best treasures are the kind that snore . . .

And how snoring can be quite . . .

                  contagioussszzzzzz . . .

                                  zzzzz . . .

Then they snored and they dreamed . . .

about a bear and a bird.